The
ROCK
Generation

6 Decades of Decline

The
ROCK
Generation

6 Decades of Decline

Frank Garlock

MAJESTY MUSIC®

Primary editor: Gina Green
Assistant editors: Shelly Hamilton, George Eastergard,
Flay Allen, Rajeesh Ghandi
Cover and book layout: David Bonikowsky

Copyright © 2018 by Frank Garlock
fgmusicman@gmail.com
All rights reserved. Printed in USA.
ISBN: 978-0-9993546-1-2

Published by Sierra Creation
SierraCreation
www.sierracreation.com

"DECLINE"

a downward slope;
a decrease in value and quality;
a diminishment in strength or quality;
a deterioration

PREFACE

The basic purpose of the book you have in your hands is to show how rock music has been one of the primary contributing factors in changing the values, the standards, the beliefs, and the basic character of a whole generation.

The last six decades have normalized rebellion, strange clothing, immodest dress for both sexes, fashions borrowed from prisons and other marginalized social groups, odd haircuts, gross toys, suggestive games, and a lifestyle that is anything but decent or Christian. The performers and promoters of the Rock genre have led the way in being a paradigm to lead a whole generation in the wrong direction. Coming at this subject from the perspective of a musician, a Bible preacher, and a concerned Christian has compelled me to put what I have observed in the last six decades into print.

I have seen the early trends of the hippies in the 1960's progress into a downward spiral of punk rock, glam rock, disco rock, hard rock, and heavy metal just to mention a few of the variations that have occurred. To make matters worse, all of these vulgar expressions of worldliness have influenced and gravitated into what is now called Contemporary Christian Music.

Many "Contemporary Christian" musicians dress like the world and use worldly, vulgar language. Their rock music overpowers even the Scripture some of them use so that it sounds like blasphemy. If this sounds farfetched to you, get on Google and look up Integrity Music (just one example), and then play what they call music. The sensual, worldly sound of the CCM performers causes them to appear to be using the name of our Savior as a swear word.

In the process, the youth culture has gotten younger and at the same time it has reached into mid-age so that many adults still act and think like adolescents. We now have forty-year-old punks; sixty-year-old hippies; men of all ages becoming trapped by pornography; and women abandoning their role as mothers in attempting to still live like a teenager, including having an abortion because of the "inconvenience" that motherhood brings.

The world keeps getting worse, as the Apostle Paul warned: "Evil men and seducers shall wax worse and worse, deceiving and being deceived" (II Timothy 3:13). Keep in mind that the Bible also admonishes us that "the path of the just is as a shining light that shineth more and more unto the perfect day" (Proverbs 4:18). The darker the world becomes the brighter our spiritual light should be.

That is why I have taken the time to do the research necessary, and to write and rewrite the material in order to try to keep the analysis concise and yet effective. It is deliberately divided into small sections to make it easier to read and digest. The format also makes a particular section easier to find when sharing it with someone else. I included a "Subject List" with page numbers so you will not need to go back and search through the whole book in order to find a particular subject.

At the suggestion of several of my trusted friends, I have closed the book with several positive, encouraging things. I trust the Bible illustrations of individuals who lived in times similar to The Rock Generation, and who followed the light they had and let God use them to influence their generation, will encourage us all to follow their example.

Praise the Lord that there are still people today who want to do the same thing in this 21st century as we look forward with anticipation to the Second Coming of our Savior. Let's remind each other of how the book of Revelation closes with these words in chapter 22, verses 21-22:

> *He which testifieth these things saith,*
> *Surely I come quickly. Amen.*
> *Even so, come, Lord Jesus!*
>
> *The grace of our Lord Jesus Christ*
> *be with you all. Amen.*

SUBJECT LIST

CONTRASTS

In 1999, Tom Brokaw wrote and compiled a book about the generation which was involved in the Second World War and called it *The Greatest Generation Speaks*.[1] The book is a fascinating account of the sacrifices that so many young Americans made to keep America safe and to attempt to bring peace to the world. It is amazing to read some of the "old-fashioned virtues" that the men and families exhibited who were born during the Great Depression and then lived and died during World War II. The entire book speaks "of duty and honor, sacrifice and accomplishment."

A few quotes from this book will give a glimpse into the thinking and dedication that was a part of the character of that generation. A soldier who was a prisoner of the Japanese said, "I kept thinking, if the good Lord wanted me to get through this, I would make it. If he didn't, I wouldn't." Another said, "World War II was universally accepted by all of us who participated as 'a just war.' There was never a question

---

1 Brokaw, Tom. *The Greatest Generation Speaks: Letters and Reflections*. Random House Trade Paperbacks, 2005.

of whether or not we were on the right side." A Polish man who later became an American serviceman said, "When I look back on those war years I thank God and my mother for our survival. Fifteen million Poles never lived to see V-E Day."

A woman who was in the WAVES (Women Accepted for Volunteer Emergency Service) was given the secret job of helping build an early computer. A Navy historian said that computer was responsible for the sinking of 750 to 800 German U-boats. Developing and using it shortened the war by one to two years. The woman said, "My parents died never knowing what I did in the service. It was a different time in our history. We were patriotic, disciplined, caring, and just so thrilled to know we were doing something special to help end the war. We never sought recognition."

Contrast what was just quoted with what has happened to the generation that has followed *The Greatest Generation*. There have been many factors that have actually spawned the demise of character and dedication, and some of these factors will be mentioned. However, one of the things that has not only revealed but contributed to problems of *The Rock Generation* is the influence of what is generally called Rock Music. Allan Bloom, in his quintessential 1987 book *The Closing of the American Mind*,[2] succinctly said, "Nothing is more singular about this generation than its **addiction to music**." Those who have lived through the last six decades of this addiction have witnessed things that never could have been imagined were possible. Bruce Rosenau was a second-

---

2 Bloom, Allan. *The Closing of the American Mind.* Simon and Schuster, 1987.

generation missionary to the Central African Republic. He was born there in 1926 and lived there most of his life. On one of his trips to the United States in 1980, he said, "What I used to see as a child in Africa, I see as an adult in America: **drugs, nudity, and hard rock**. There was one village near us that was given over to marijuana so that we could not reach it with the gospel." This missionary was saying he believed that by 1980 the United States had already retrogressed to the heathenism he witnessed in Africa.

A Cultural Chasm

A perusal of the songs of *The Greatest Generation* indicates the great cultural chasm that occurred between that generation and *The Rock Generation* that was to come in like a tsunami in the 1960's. Here is a short list of songs written and made popular by *The Greatest Generation*. Some of these songs were recorded many times by different artists, and their popularity reveals the dramatic difference between their generation and *The Rock Generation*: "God Bless America;"[1] "I Only Have Eyes for You;"[2] "I'll Be Loving You, Always;"[3] "I Left My Heart in San Francisco;"[4] "I'll See You Again;"[5] "Thine Alone;"[6] "All the Things You Are;"[7] "One Kiss, One Man to Save It For;"[8]

---

1 Berlin, Irving. "God Bless America," 1938. Famously sung by Kate Smith, "The First Lady of Radio."

2 Warren, Harry, and Al Dubin. "I Only Have Eyes for You," 1934.

3 Berlin, Irving. "Always," 1925.

4 Cory, George, and Douglass Cross. "I Left My Heart in San Francisco," 1953.

5 Coward, Noël. "I'll See You Again," 1929.

6 Herbert, Victor, and Henry Blossom. "Thine Alone," 1917.

7 Kern, Jerome, and Oscar Hammerstein. "All the Things You Are," 1939.

8 Romberg, Sigmund, and Oscar Hammerstein. "One Kiss," 1927.

and many, many more. These songs expressed commitment, patriotism, dedication to a cause or to another person, what it means to really be in love, the real meaning of love and romance, civility and decorum, maturity and responsibility, even perspective and wisdom.

In addition to this, the music itself expressed the values that accompany "good music"— music that has a past and is built on the principles of good, well-trained composers, such as Oscar Hammerstein, Sigmund Romberg, Morton Gould, Richard Rogers, Alan Jay Lerner, Aaron Copeland, Robert Russell Bennett, Leroy Anderson, and many others of *The Greatest Generation*. Their music was melody-driven, not beat-driven, and the music itself accurately portrayed the words or the message that it was accompanying.

A TEMPER TANTRUM

Anyone reading this may want to obtain a copy of *The Death of the Grown-Up* by Diana West.[1] This book was published in 2007 and details the degradation that ensued as the children of *The Greatest Generation* became a generation of "**eternal adolescents**." For instance, on page 56, West details what happened during that period of decadence. Referring to the previous generation, she says that they "didn't shrink from an invading army, an invading people, or an invading ideology. It *retreated* from the ultimate 'enemy within': **its own children**."

And then on page 59, she makes this revealing observation: "It's a safe bet that Ivy Alumni at that same Harvard–Princeton matchup, circa, say, 1959 — and certainly 1949 and earlier — would have slapped down any youth movement attempting to make policy in the streets." Between pages 26 and 45, at least a dozen times West mentions **rock 'n' roll** as a major contributing factor to this degradation that she calls "**the biggest temper tantrum in the history of the world**."

---

1 West, Diana. *The Death of the Grown-up: How America's Arrested Development Is Bringing down Western Civilization.* St. Martin's Press, 2007.

In 1949 Dr. H. A. Ironside spoke at the Bob Jones University Spring Bible Conference. His text was I Thessalonians 4:13. That day he prophetically said in a humorous manner: "We have had the Plymouth Brethren, The Grace Brethren, The United Brethren, and now we have THE IGNORANT BRETHREN." *The Rock Generation* is a present-day example of Dr. Ironside's satire.

THE NARCOTIZATION OF SIN

Sin blinds! This principle is stated very clearly in the Word of God, and it can even happen to Christians. After giving a list of virtues that Christians are to "add to [their] faith," the Apostle Peter in his second general epistle says, "He that lacketh these things is blind, and cannot see afar off, and hath forgotten that he was purged from his old sins" (II Peter 1:9). Remember that this is referring to born-again people, and if it can even happen to Christians, no one should be surprised that intelligent unsaved people are so blind concerning the difference between right and wrong, truth and error, and good and evil (Isaiah 5:20). Sin acts like a narcotic that affects every part of a person's life so that it addicts and intoxicates to such a degree that the mind cannot reason clearly.

In his book *Not the Way It's Supposed to Be: A Breviary of Sin*, Cornelius Plantinga, Jr. effectively uses the metaphor of music to describe the results of sin:[1]

---

1 Plantinga, Cornelius. *Not the Way It's Supposed to Be: a Breviary of Sin*. Eerdmans, 1999.

Self-deception about our sin is a narcotic, a tranquilizing and disorienting suppression of our central nervous system. What's devastating about it is that when we lack an ear for wrong notes in our lives, we cannot play right notes or even recognize them in the performance of others."

What Plantinga goes on to say about that anesthetizing process is that it leads us to become religiously unmusical. One will need to search a long time to find a clearer description of how music teaches the principles of life and the consequences of sin that God has given in His Word.

⸺ 🌀 ⸺

PERILOUS TIMES

The twenty-first century is witnessing a generation that is "having a form of godliness, but denying the power thereof" (II Timothy 3:5). The description that Apostle Paul gives at the beginning of that Scripture accurately portrays what can now be called *The Rock Generation*. Paul's list describes 18 characteristics of a generation that will be living "in the last days [when] perilous times shall come."

Here is the list that sounds like what is being experienced today: "Lovers of themselves, lovers of money, boasters, proud, blasphemers, disobedient to parents, unthankful, unholy, unloving, unforgiving, slanderers, without self-control, brutal, despisers of good, traitors, headstrong, haughty, [and] lovers of pleasure rather than lovers of God" (II Timothy 3:1-5). All these things have been true through the ages, but they have been *intensified* in the six decades of *The Rock Generation*. However, not only have characteristics of "perilous times" intensified during *The Rock Generation*, the devil now has more *resources* that he can use to tempt and trap people. For instance, computers and cellular phones are a tremendous benefit, but they are also making pornography and other impropriety more readily available than ever before.

All one needs to do is grasp what Marshall McLuhan and Wilson Bryan Key, both of whom were philosophers of what was called "Communication Theory," said almost 50 years ago: "If you don't believe what I am saying about what is happening, just look out the window!" In other words, look at what is happening around you and you will know that there are factors which are causing certain things to come to pass.

MUSICAL STYLE

At the time when these philosophers were saying this, Majesty Music applied what was then considered their "controversial" teaching to what was fast becoming the popular music of the day: rock. MM paraphrased McLuhan's "the medium is the massage," and called it "the *music* is the *message!*" We even went so far as to say in 1965: "If you will tell us what kind of music you listen to and the kind of music you like, we will tell you what kind of person you are."

Interestingly, in the July 1999 issue of *Christianity Today*, there was an article titled "The Triumph of the Praise Songs," in which Michael S. Hamilton says:[1] "When one chooses a musical **style** today, one is making a statement about whom one identifies with, what one's values are, and ultimately, WHO ONE IS." Notice that this author believes it is "musical style" that reveals identity, values, and character or individuality.

---

1 Hamilton, Michael S. "The Triumph of the Praise Song." *Christianity Today*, vol. 43, no. 8, 12 July 1999, www. christianitytoday.com/ct/1999/july12/9t8028.html.

This is a reflection of what Neil Postman said in his book, *Amusing Ourselves to Death* in 1985:[1] "The form in which ideas are expressed affects what those ideas will be." In other words, music is an indicator or a barometer of what is happening in a given society, and this is true of churches as well. The music that a church chooses and its people desire for "worship" shows what is happening in that church and indicates the direction that church is headed.

1 Postman, Neil. *Amusing Ourselves to Death: Public Discourse in the Age of Show Business.* Viking Books, 1985.

MUSIC IS AN INDICATOR

The quintessential passage of Scripture that illustrates this principle is Exodus 32:15-28. Moses and Joshua had gone up Mount Sinai to receive instructions from the Lord, including the Ten Commandments. As they are coming down, they hear the sound coming from the camp below. Joshua believes it is the sound of *war* (verse 17). Moses recognizes that it is the "noise of them that *sing* do I hear" (verse 18). When Moses then saw the dancing and the calf, he broke the tables of stone, engraved by God, that he had been carrying.

This is also another illustration of the blindness of sin. When Moses asked Aaron where the calf came from, (that Aaron himself had engraved), Aaron basically said: "I threw the gold that the people gave me into the fire, and out came this calf." How imbecilic can an excuse be?!

However, God's ancillary purpose of this passage appears to be to show how music indicates what is actually going on in a place where they say they are worshipping Him. Aaron had told the people they were going to have "a feast to the LORD!" (verse 5). What God called *corruption* (verse 7), Aaron said they were going use *that same music* and *sensual dancing* to worship the LORD. However, the music that Moses heard coming from the camp indicated to him how terrible the sin of the people was. This applies to most Contemporary Christian Music today. Churches are using the devil's sensual music and say they are worshiping God.

Defining Rock Music

There is a general temptation among many Christians today to lump anything they don't personally like and call it "rock music." I want to be clear in defining what rock music is. I believe the most accurate way is to see what the people who make and promote "rock music" say about it. Looking at the quotes in this book by these people reveals the elements that define rock.

This first quote is from a Juilliard School of Music student who liked rock, and who was interviewed by the New York Times and quoted in High Fidelity magazine.[1] Notice what he said:

> *The problem with rock is that its defining limits are VISCERAL rather than CEREBRAL. It is a visceral form of expression, and VOLUME is often used to cover up lack of techniques.*

1 Peyser, Joan. "The Coming Generation of Musicians." *High Fidelity*, Apr. 1972.

This man who became a professional musician gave insight into the basic problems with rock. *Visceral* means relating to the internal organs of the body, and it could be translated earthy, crude, or coarse. It is a fast automatic reaction that is non-intellectual. *Cerebral* means an emotional reaction that is conscious and involves participation of the intellect.

To approach visceral and cerebral from a spiritual standpoint: one means appealing to the flesh and the other means appealing to the spirit. "The flesh lusts against the spirit, and the spirit lusts against the flesh; and these are contrary the one to the other" (Galatians 5:17). When he talks about the volume covering up techniques, he is inadvertently referring to how the loudness overpowers the message.

The most concise definition of rock comes from Chuck Berry, a champion of rock music, who defines rock as: "***The beat of the drums loud and bold***." Without realizing it, Berry reveals the three basic elements that define rock. Number one is the **beat**. All good music has a variety of rhythms, but rock has an overwhelming beat of the drums. This constant emphasis on the beat is one of the main elements of rock. Good music always emphasizes melody and harmony. Rock is a tedious cycle of short phrases and constantly repeated chords.

Number two that Berry mentions is that rock is **loud**!! Many comparisons to volume are mentioned later in this book, but there is no question about the fact that it is **loud**. Drive your car anywhere near another car that is playing rock and you will not only hear the sound, but feel it in your car. The same thing is true in any place that plays rock; it is always **loud**!

Berry's number three is that rock is **bold**!! No other music has ever captivated a civilization like the way rock has hypnotized the rock generation. Look at the strong adjectives that its proponents and participants use to describe it: **addicting, rebellious, nihilistic, a temper tantrum, a lifestyle of drugs and alcohol, acid rock, punk rock, heavy metal, etc. & etc**.

Exodus 32:6 tells what part of rock makes its proponents use the previous adjectives. The Hebrew word for "play" in that verse is a similar word used in Deuteronomy 22:21 to describe what a harlot does when she entices: she "plays." Rock music has induced thousands of susceptible, naïve girls to imitate prostitutes by the way they move their bodies to rock music.

It is not only the performers who simulate and pantomime portrayals of promiscuous sexuality and pornography. Watch the motions that anyone goes through while listening to most rock and you must know that rock is **sensual**. Bands that march down the street don't move like that; orchestras and performers of classical music don't move like that; only rock elicits twerking and other disgustingly indecent and sensual suggestiveness.

Another element that defines the effects of rock music is what has been known for centuries as "**sympathetic vibration**." This was part of what made David's harp playing effective with King Saul that is still being used in hospitals today. The entire harp vibrates sympathetically with each string like no other instrument does.

This principle applies to people and the kind of music they like and respond to. In *Rock and Roll: A Social History*,[1] Paul Friedlander says that the lifestyle of a large number of rock performers has resulted in death by drug overdose and suicide. This man, who praises rock and its performers, has to admit that their **style of music** is in sympathetic vibration with their **lifestyle**. The kind of music that a person likes shows what kind of person he or she is. Rock and rebellion appear to be co-conspirators in reckless self-destruction.

1 Friedlander, Paul. *Rock and Roll: A Social History*. Westview, 1996.

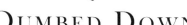

DUMBED DOWN

Another problem that must be faced in these "perilous times" is that the thinking of many people has been "dumbed down" to such a degree that they really cannot think clearly or logically. This is particularly obvious in the political arena where a president, many liberal senators and members of the House of Representatives believed the country could lower its debt by taxing the people more and more. A check of the education background of these people reveals that they graduated from Ivy League schools and other colleges in the 1970s and 1980s. These institutions were at the center of protests and liberalism during *The Rock Generation*. This anti-intellectualism and inability to think logically has been promoted in rock for a long time. For instance, the Punk Rock Ramones in 1979 sang:[2]

> *I don't care about history;*
> *That's not where I want to be—*
> *I just wanna have some kicks.*

---

2 Ramone, Dee Dee, et al. "Rock 'n' Roll High School," 1979.

Chuck Berry expressed the same anti-intellectual theme in *School Days* in 1957 in what could be considered the Rock 'n' Roll anthem:[1]

> *Hail, hail, rock 'n' roll,*
> *Deliver me from the days of old.*
> *Long live rock 'n' roll,*
> *The beat of the drums loud and bold.*

Robert Pattison in his 1987 book *The Triumph of Vulgarity*, page 141 says:[2]

> *Rock lyrics are suffused with the language of emotion: Need, want, and feel are the building blocks of its abstract vocabulary. Logic and reason are everywhere associated with the loss of youth and the death of vitality.*

On page 89 of his book, Pattison goes on to say:

> *When the pantheist equates self and God, he demotes thought to a secondary role in the universe and elevates feeling as the fundamental way of knowing.*

1 Berry, Chuck. "School Days," 1957.

2 Pattison, Robert. *The Triumph of Vulgarity: Rock Music in the Mirror of Romanticism.* Oxford UP, 1987.

Dumbed Down Christian Music

What the previous quotes say applies to the singing in many churches today in a dramatic way. Go to almost any church and listen to the congregational and the choir singing as well. They don't sing in parts any more. Everyone sings the melody if there is much of a melody. It quite often just "wanders around" and never seems to get anywhere.

Sixty-five years ago, many Christians thought that the Christian-School movement was going to be the answer for the next generation. That has not materialized in either theology or music. In fact, so many Christian schools today no longer even offer music training. The administrations contend they don't have the money to hire music teachers, but they do hire athletic directors, and sports have become their main emphasis. This has resulted in a *dumbing down* of Christian music so that many churches no longer have choirs, they no longer use hymnbooks, and the music is a cheap imitation of what the world uses.

Martin Luther, whose musical skill was considerable, is remembered for his ability in both theology and music. He was not only a lover of music but also a proficient musician. Luther believed that the reformation was not complete until the saints of God had two things in their possession: a Bible in their own tongue, and a hymnal. The hymnal was called the Psalter because the words were based on the Psalms. Luther's critics said "the *people* were singing themselves into the Lutheran doctrine." They did this by teaching the people how to sing hymns with the music in four parts, not the Gregorian chant which was not sung by the congregation. Here is a quote from Martin Luther himself:[1]

> *These songs have been set **in four parts** for no other reason than because I wished to provide our young people (who both will and ought to be instructed in music and other sciences) with something whereby they might rid themselves of amorous and carnal songs, and in their stead learn something wholesome.*

He believed that because the music was to be the servant of the words and to enhance them, the music must not be associated with activities and things opposed to the purity of the Christian life. He also wanted the music he wrote to accurately "portray" the words of the text, as in "A Mighty Fortress." Luther's success in his endeavor is shown by the widespread use of his chorales in worship services even today."

---

1 Luther, Martin. *Eyn Geystlich Gesangk Buchleyn.* Johann
  Walter, 1524. Called the First Wittenberg Hymnal.

If you are interested in seeing an example of contemporary excellent hymn writing, look up vignette 19 in *Just Show Up: God Can Use You*, where words by Dr. Bob Jones Jr. were skillfully set to music by Joan Pinkston.[2]

---

2 Garlock, Frank. *Just Show Up: God Can Use You*. Sierra Creation, 2017.

DISCERNMENT

In a 2002 book called *Who Needs Classical Music* by Julian Johnson,[1] the author makes the observation that consternation is caused for "those who believe that the intensity of their own emotional response is sufficient proof of the music's quality and therefore authenticity, but this is no truer of music than it is of other symbolic languages."

Johnson then goes on to say: "**When the emotional responses aroused by political orators have been taken as a measure of their truth, social disaster has usually ensued**." Mr. Johnson's words are a prime example of what is happening politically in the United States today!

Take, for example, an article written for the "Rochester Review" of the University of Rochester by Paul R. Gross, dean of graduate studies at the UR.[2] This article was titled "Beware

---

1 Johnson, Julian. *Who Needs Classical Music? Cultural Choice and Musical Value*. Oxford UP, 2002.

2 Gross, Paul R. "Beware the Illusion of Learning." *Rochester Review*, 1975, www.lib.rochester.edu/IN/RBSCP/Databases/Attachments/Reviews/1975/38-1/1975_Fall.pdf.

the Illusion of Learning" and it critiques a convention of Medical Educators that was held in Miami Beach in 1973. In attendance were 55 psychiatrists, psychologists, and social workers who were to listen to a speaker named Doctor Myron L. Fox and judge his effectiveness as a communicator. "Doctor Fox" was actually **an actor** who gave "a carefully concocted tissue of nonsense, ambiguity, contradictions and non sequitur. " ALL of the medical educators in attendance "rated him very highly on each of the six key elements of contribution to good learning." Not one person realized they had been duped by an actor "who looked distinguished and sounded authoritative." These highly educated people thought they had learned something from a lecture with "no substantive truth."

Loud Music

There is a great deal of recent research that documents what Dr. Gross delineated concerning the lack of discernment among even educated people who allow themselves to be addicted to what is called rock music. There are several reports that verify the fact that music, and particularly "loud music" can alter people's brains and make them susceptible to philosophies and ideas that do not make any sense. Remember that Dr. Gross wrote his article from a university campus in 1975 when rock music was flourishing everywhere and its influence was being felt extensively.

Perhaps it would be wise to define what is meant by "loud music" at this point. Sound power, or acoustic power, is a measure of sonic energy, and it can be expressed in watts, which is a measurement of amplitude over time. Watts can also be used to compute sound intensity. While power is measured in watts, the most-used acoustic measurement for intensity is the decibel. (On the logarithmic scale, unlike an arithmetic scale, the acoustic measure of the sound is doubled for every increase of just three decibels.) Without becoming too technical, here are some examples of loudness that the average person should be able to understand. (Anyone who wants more detailed information should just put "Loud Music" into Google and watch what comes up.)

God is the Creator who has made even the heavens with what can be called musical principles. Albert Einstein said that "without a belief in the inner harmony of the universe, there would be no science at all." For instance, scientists have discovered a "black hole" in space that "sings a B-flat" that is 57 octaves below middle C on a piano. One would imagine that the sound would be deafening to our ears. But scientists who discovered the black hole declare that "the intensity of the sound is *comparable to human speech*." Since God calls all the stars "by their names" (Psalm 147:4), it would appear that the sounds they make are similar in intensity to the voice of a human being and would not hurt anyone's ears.

COMPARISONS

However, coming back to scholarly reports about music principles can help us to understand what is meant by "loud music." Recognizing the variables like distance from the origin of the sound and the consonance or dissonance of the sound, if there is no artificial amplification, a violin generates one-twentieth of a watt, a trombone generates about 6 watts, and a full orchestra about 67 watts. None of these sounds will damage anyone's eardrums.

Approaching the subject from another angle, a high-end home system usually has about 150 watts, a good church sound system has about 250 watts, and a large auditorium has about 3,000 watts. However, Mickey Hart (the drummer for the rock group called "The Grateful Dead") has what he calls a "beam" (a ten-foot aluminum girder) that is fed into an amplifier that generates 170,000 watts of sound. This is right on the edge of what is called "the threshold of pain," and acousticians declare that that much sound creates "*instant permanent hearing damage.*"

Now it is obvious that not many rock concerts generate as much sound as Mickey Hart does. But rock bands employ amplifiers that greatly exceed the limit of the sound God intended anyone's ears to be exposed to safely absorb. Yet many churches also generate sound levels that acoustic scientists say damage ears in less than 15 minutes. What follows is a current example which shows what is happening to the sound level in some churches, not just in rock concerts. This is happening in the sixth decade of *The Rock Generation*.

A PUBLIC NUISANCE

On Sunday, March 17, 2013, *The Greenville News[1]* printed an article about a church in Columbia, South Carolina that has received "at least 16 tickets" for violating the law that states that using "any instrument or sound-producing or sound-amplifying device so loudly as to unreasonably disturb persons in the vicinity… renders the instrument or device **a public nuisance**." Officers must come inside the house next door to the church "to verify an unreasonable level of noise before writing a ticket." The police chief says, "You don't hear it. You feel it. This is a very serious issue."

In 1997, Robert Jourdain wrote a fascinating and insightful book: *Music, the Brain and Ecstasy.[2]* In his book, Jourdain examines how music speaks in ways that words cannot. He deals in detail with every aspect of music including sound, tone, melody, harmony, rhythm, composition, listening, and understanding. In addressing the issue of volume, he writes: "Music has always been about not hurting ears."

---

1 "Pentecostal Church's Neighbors Find Little Cause for Rejoicing." *The Greenville News*, 17 Mar. 2013, www.newspapers.com/newspage/108956472/.

2 Jourdain, Robert. *Music, the Brain, and Ecstasy: How Music Captures Our Imagination*. William Morrow, 1997.

Addiction

Barry Blesser, Ph.D., in his 2007 article "The Seductive (Yet Destructive) Appeal of Loud Music"[3] states, "The scientific literature unequivocally proves that prolonged exposure to loud sound produces permanent damage to the hair cells in the inner ear… There is no question that loud music can significantly change the mind body state… Loud music has also been implicated in psychological disorientation… Loud music activated those brain regions that are associated with euphoric drugs, such as cocaine… Loud music exhibited maladaptive behavior patterns consistent with drug abuse… **Like every drug, loud music can be destructive**."

A few years before this, there was a fascinating article called "Take Two Tunes and Call Me in the Morning,"[4] because doctors are seeing a connection between harmonious, soothing sound and health. This article in USA WEEKEND of December 17-19, 1999, quotes Pierce J. Howard, Ph.D., the author of *The Owner's Manual for the Brain*: "Very loud music

---

3 Barry Blesser. "The Seductive (Yet Destructive) Appeal of Loud Music."
EContact!, vol. 9, no. 4, June 2007, econtact.ca/9_4/blesser.html.

4 "Take Two Tunes and Call Me in the Morning."
USA Weekend, 17 Dec. 1999.

creates an altered state of consciousness **akin to an alcoholic or drug-induced stupor that can become addictive.**"[1]

It must be understood that rock or CCM music is not the only thing that has molded the thinking and values of *The Rock Generation*. However, it is definitely one of the major factors that have taken the prevailing mindset of that generation away from biblical truth. II Timothy 3:7 characterizes those who only have a form of godliness as "ever learning, and never able to come to the knowledge of the truth." And the first chapter of Romans says they "hold the truth in unrighteousness… professing themselves to be wise, they became fools" (Romans 1:18, 22).

This book is not a duplication of the quintessential book that my daughter, Shelly Hamilton, has recently written. Hers is an excellent book that will help any reader who wants to know what is behind the title of her book: *Why I Don't Listen to Contemporary Christian Music.*[2] Shelly deals with facts and documentation and not with personal preferences or individual tastes. Her book should be read by anyone who wants to know the truth about the roots and influences of what is now called CCM. What is being addressed here is how Rock Music has changed the values, the standards, the beliefs, and the basic character of a whole generation.

---

1 Howard, Pierce J. *The Owner's Manual for the Brain: Everyday Applications from Mind-Brain Research.* Bard Press, 1999.

2 Hamilton, Shelly. *Why I Don't Listen to Contemporary Christian Music.* Majesty Music, 2013.

GENERATION TO GENERATION

Scripture is very emphatic in instructing God's people to preserve God's standards from generation to generation. For instance, God told Moses to write a song and "teach it to the children of Israel: put it in their mouths... for it shall not be forgotten out of the mouths of their seed [descendants]" (Deuteronomy 31:19, 21).

Psalm 71:18 is an excellent verse to use and apply for anyone who has lived through the last six decades: "Now also when I am old and grayheaded, O God, forsake me not; until I have showed thy strength unto this generation, and thy power to everyone that is to come."

A classic passage in Psalm 78:3-7 tells of the importance of every generation passing the torch of Truth to the next generation: "[That] which we have heard and known, and our fathers have told us, we will not hide them from their children, showing the generation to come the praises of the LORD, and his strength, and his wonderful works that he hath done... that they should make them known to their children: that the generation to come might know them, even the children which should be born; who should arise and declare them to their children; that they might set their hope in God, and forget not the works of God, but keep his commandments."

Somehow the inherent value of God's calling upon our lives has not been communicated to the present generation, and they have become a generation that does not seem to know God as they should. For instance, at the graduation exercises of a Christian high school several years ago, it was amazing that not only were none of the graduates planning to go to a Christian college, but none of them were planning to go into any of the areas that are called Christian service. When the pastor and principal of the Christian school were asked why this was the case, their reply was: "Not everyone is called into the Lord's service." However, if their leaders are doing their job right, and living a good testimony before the students, SOMEONE SHOULD BE!

In the fall season of 2017, a new survey of millennials (people in their 20s and 30s) discovered that "nearly 45% of millennials in the U.S. say they would rather live in a socialist country than in a 'capitalist democracy.'"[1] In addition to that, "7% of millennials would rather live under a Communist regime" than where they live now. Twenty percent of them believe that Stalin was a hero, and 25% believe that Lenin also was. They also believe that the murderous despot, North Korean Kim Jong Un is a hero.

---

1 Victims of Communism Memorial Foundation. "Annual Report on US Attitudes Toward Socialism." Survey. October, 2017. victimsofcommunism.org/wp-content/uploads/2017/11/YouGov-VOC-2017-for-Media-Release-November-2-2017-final.pdf

It should be obvious that the college professors of today are brainwashing these young people who cannot think logically because of their addiction to rock music. Their college professors were likely the rebels of the 1960s through the 1980s who listened to rock and possibly took the drugs that are affecting their minds now. 97% of the history professors in the Ivy-League schools are liberals who voted for the ultra-liberal Hillary Clinton for president.

Obviously, there are exceptions and it is encouraging to meet and know young people who want to live for the Lord and serve Him with their hearts and lives. The older generation should take advantage of the technology that is available today to pray and encourage any young people who are seeking God's will for their individual lives.

MAJESTY MUSIC

Majesty Music has been involved in educating Christians about these problems for much of the six decades of *The Rock Generation*. Messages for teenagers were developed in 1965, produced in an album called The Big Beat: A Rock Blast in 1969-70, and in a book by the same title in 1971.[1] The next project was a series of messages called *Symphony of Life Seminar* that was recorded on a set of cassettes in 1984. In 1992, those messages were updated, video recorded, and renamed *The Language of Music*, and translated into Spanish. In 2003, when churches wanted one day seminars, usually Sunday, a shortened version was produced and called *Pop Goes the Music*. Then in 2008 one more three-video set was developed and called *The Nature of Music*. Along the way, several pamphlets that addressed current issues were printed, including: *Jesus Christ Superstar—Blessing or Blasphemy,*[2] *Can Rock Music Be Sacred?*[3] and *Is CCM a Cultural Thing?*[4]

---

1 Garlock, Frank. *The Big Beat: a Rock Blast*. BJU Press, 1971.

2 Garlock, Frank. *Jesus Christ Superstar: Blessing or Blasphemy?* BJU Press, 1971.

3 Garlock, Frank. *Can Rock Music Be Sacred?* Musical Minsitries, 1974.

4 Garlock, Frank. "Is CCM a Cultural Thing?" *Frontline Magazine*, 2004, fbfi.org/wp-content/uploads/2017/01/2004.04.FrontLine.pdf.

"IMAGINE"

At this point, a synopsis of a journey through the songs of *The Rock Generation* should demonstrate how the songs of each of the last six decades have contributed to the degeneration that is being experienced in the twenty-first century. It will not be a pleasant journey any more than it has been pleasant to do the research that was necessary. The motivation and desire for this book is to address what has happened to the current generation and how that has influenced many of the people who call themselves Christians. In 1971, John Lennon of the Beatles wrote a song called "Imagine," that without his realizing it, expresses what the world and this generation of "Christians" believes:[5]

> *"Imagine there's no heaven, it's easy if you try;*
> *No hell beneath us, above us only sky.*
> *Imagine all the people living for today."*

If you think "Imagine" portrayed something that was only in vogue 48 years ago, you are mistaken. Remember that

---

5 Lennon, John, and Yoko Ono. "Imagine," 1971.

"Imagine" has sold more than 1.6 million copies. It was played just before the New York Times Square Ball fell in New York City in 2005. It also opened the 2006 Winter Olympics in Torino, Italy. Then it was played during the end credits at the close of the 2012 Summer Olympics. This world-wide exposure and fascination appears to indicate that the whole world is not only singing this godless anti-biblical philosophy, but has embraced it.

An article titled "Pop Goes Christianity"[1] in Slate Magazine, a liberal online current affairs and culture magazine owned by the Washington Post Company, stated that "In the 80's, Christians embarked on the curious quest to enlist America's crassest materials culture in the service of spiritual growth… **You shoehorn a message that's essentially about obeying authority into a genre that's rebellious and nihilistic, and the result can be ugly**… It's more like an eternal oxymoron."

James Montgomery Boice hit the nail on the head in 1991 when he wrote: "We invent religion—not because we are seeking God, but because we are running away from Him."[2] In 1957, William Culbertson voiced the same sentiment from a different perspective: "If a man travels far enough away from Christianity, he is always in danger of seeing it in perspective and deciding that it is true. It is much safer, from Satan's point

1 Rosin, Hanna. "Pop Goes Christianity." *Slate Magazine*, 5 May 2008, www.slate.com/articles/arts/books/2008/05/pop_goes_christianity.html.

2 Boice, J.M. *Romans*. Vol. 1, Baker, 1991.

of view, to vaccinate a man with a mild dose of Christianity, so as to protect him from the real thing."[3]

3 Culbertson, William. "Taking the Cross and Following the Lord." *The Keswick Week 1957*, R. W. Simpson, 1957. evan-logan-92k5.squarespace.com/s/1957_keswick.pdf

NOTIONAL CHRISTIANS

Here are some statistics from the Barna Research Group as reported in an article titled "Christian Teens? Not Very!" in the Wall Street Journal in July 9, 2004.[1] "Mushy doctrine among the younger generation ranks as the No. 1 crisis facing American Christendom today!... Americans today are intellectually and spiritually frivolous."

- 88% of teens say they are Christians, but 53% believe that Jesus committed sins while He was here on this earth.
- 62% "who call themselves Christians" believe the Bible is totally accurate, but only 9% of "born-again teens" believe in moral absolutes.
- 60% of evangelical Christian teenagers now say that all religious faiths teach equally valid truths.
- 61% agree that "if a person is generally good, or does enough good things for others during their life, they will earn a place in Heaven."

---

1 Buss, Dale. "Christian Teens? Not Very." *Wall Street Journal*, 9 July 2004, www.wsj.com/articles/SB108932505338159136.

Barna then refers to what are called **Notional Christians**: "Those who describe themselves as Christians, and believe they will have eternal life, but *not* because of a grace-based relationship with Jesus Christ." Barna said they represented 39% of the population in 2004. If this was true in 2004, think what it must be now! It is also interesting to note that in the 2016 national election, evangelicals gave Trump 79% and only 18% to Clinton. By contrast, the Notional Christians only gave Trump 49%, and 47% to Clinton, virtually 50-50, similar to the Catholic vote.

Dale Buss, a writer for the *Wall Street Journal* goes on to say: "It's disconcerting that we're relying on this generation for the future defense of Judeo-Christian civilization against the highly-motivated forces of militant Islam. It reflects **a pseudo-faith** that is fed by a steady diet of pop-culture feints." Buss does not mention it, but that includes music.

BLASPHEMY AND REBELLION

When *Jesus Christ Superstar*, written by Tim Rice and Andrew Lloyd Webber in 1970, was performed in Greenville, South Carolina in 2003, *The Greenville News* received many letters with sentiments like the following one: "I am a Christian… and Superstar built my faith." Rice and Webber both said they were writing Superstar to show that Jesus was "a mixed-up man like Judas." The song "I Don't Know How to Love Him" has Mary Magdalene (a prostitute in the opera) say this about Jesus:[1]

> *"He's a man, he's just a man,*
> *And I've had so many men before;*
> *In very many ways, he's just one more."*

What kind of Christians, especially in "The Bible Belt," would believe that a song like that could build their faith?

Consider what Mark Stuart, the lead singer of "Audio Adrenaline" (a veteran CCM group), was quoted as saying in

---

1 Webber, Andrew Lloyd, and Tim Rice. "I Don't Know How to Love Him," 1970.

Newsweek magazine on July 15, 2001:[2] "I think rebellion and Christianity go together. Christianity is about rebellion. Jesus Christ is the biggest rebel to ever walk the face of the earth. He was crucified for his rebellion... Rock 'n' roll is about the same thing—rebellion." Stuart recognizes that Rock is rebellion, but he says that is OK because his kind of "Christianity" also promotes rebellion.

That same Newsweek magazine that bore the headline "Jesus Rocks" said that 50,000 teens came together to "wreak havoc and give praise. The kids have the option to visit the prayer area if they're not moshing." A mosh pit is a place of "controlled violence," usually at the front of audience. There are various kinds of mosh pits, but they all have face-whacking, punching, slam-dancing, walloping, and other forms of masochism, including sadomasochism.

It does not take much imagination to realize why so many young people in their 20's and 30's are turning away from what they call "Christianity." Actually, there are two main reasons. Number one is they have been so mentally intoxicated by Rock Music that they are looking for an emotional "high" instead of looking for the reality of a living Savior and the infallible Truth of His Word. Number two is the high-powered music of CCM has failed to reach their hearts, and like all other drugs it has led them on a quest for something more intoxicating.

2 Ali, Lorraine. "The Glorious Rise of Christian Pop." *Newsweek*, 15 July 2001, www.newsweek.com/glorious-rise-christian-pop-154551.

WORLDLINESS

Companies that promote CCM today have followed suit in imitating secular rock that groups now not only sound just like their secular counterparts, they *look* just like them. They present a sensual image that includes outlandish jewelry, tattoos, and a countenance that makes them appear as rude and rebellious as secular punk rock and heavy metal. Their use of inappropriate language and sensual innuendos has become an accepted form of their so called "Christianity." Amy Grant admitted why she said and acted the way she did: "I'm trying to look sexy to sell a record … I feel that a Christian young woman in the 1980's is very sexy."[1]

Diana West, whom we have cited before, mentions in her book, *The Death of the Grown-Up,* that The Rock Generation creates an atmosphere "that is amoral to a point of immorality." What West says on page 11 of her book is true of many "Christians" today: **"He may not be a punk, but he'll talk that way: she may not be a slut, but she'll dress that way."**

---

1 Goldberg, Michael. "Amy Grant Wants to Put God on the Charts." *Rolling Stone*, 6 June 1985.

A False Gospel

The second reason there is a falling away among people of *The Rock Generation* is that many of them have been worshipping and following a man-made god who can never satisfy the longing of the human heart. In other words, they have the wrong god because they have never found nor had a close relationship with the God of the Bible. By contrast, Jerome Hines, a famous opera singer who sang more major roles at the Metropolitan Opera House in New York than any other singer ever has or probably ever will, said, "People say I believe in God. They are wrong. **I know Him**."[2] What a difference!!

A group of nine researchers for The Environmental Protection Agency wrote the following about the addictiveness of rock music: "One of the most powerful releases of the fight-or-flight adrenaline high is **music which is discordant in its beat or chords**. Good music follows exact mathematical rules, which cause the mind to feel comforted, encouraged, and 'safe.' Musicians have found that when they go against these rules, the listener experiences an **addicting high**."[3]

---

2 Hines, Jerome. *This Is My Story, This Is My Song.*
  Fleming H. Revel Company, 1968.

3 *Audiology Research*, vol. 2, no. 1, 2012.

DOCTORS AND OPIOIDS

Like unscrupulous 'diet' doctors who addicted their clients to amphetamines to ensure their continued dependence, musicians know that discordant music sells and sells. Many of the doctors, who were protesting, drug-taking teenagers several decades ago, have administered opioids to their patients. They are now into trouble because these "medicines" have caused an epidemic. They are giving opioids out like candy.

A recent report by the National Institutes of Health suggests that when it comes to the treatment of chronic pain, the medical profession may be very much in violation of what can be regarded as the first medical ethic: "First, do no harm." In fact, the Hippocratic Oath that all doctors are supposed to swear to states: "Nor shall any man's entreaty prevail upon me to administer poison to anyone; neither will I counsel any man to do so."

The NIH in 2018 stated that "more than 115 Americans die every day after overdosing on opioids. The misuse of and addiction to opioids—including prescription pain relievers, heroin, and synthetic opioids is a serious national crisis that affects public health as well as social and economic welfare."[1]

How does the NIH say this happened? In the late 1990s, pharmaceutical companies reassured the medical community that patients would not become addicted to prescription opioid pain relievers. In 2015, more than 33,000 Americans died as a result of an opioid overdose, including prescription opioids and heroin. That same year, an estimated two million people in the United States suffered from substance use disorders related to prescription opioid pain relievers, and 591,000 suffered from a heroin use disorder.

Here is what the NIH says they know about the opioid crisis:

- An estimated 4 to 6 percent who misuse prescription opioids transition to heroin.
- About 80 percent of people who use heroin first misused prescription opioids.

This issue has become a public health crisis with devastating consequences. President Trump is at this time scheduling conferences about the opioid epidemic. The increase in injection drug use has also contributed to the spread of infectious diseases including HIV and Hepatitis C.

---

1 "Opioid Overdose Crisis." *National Institutes of Health*, Feb. 2018, www.drugabuse.gov/drugs-abuse/opioids/opioid-overdose-crisis.

An Epidemic

There are several things that the NIH has missed about this crisis that they now face. Number one is that the addiction to drugs, and especially heroin, came because the promoters and performers of rock 'n' roll encouraged it through their songs and their lifestyles from the 1960's on, so that it has become an epidemic in the twenty-first century.

Number two is that the doctors who are now prescribing these drugs are the same people who were listening to Rock Music and became addicted to heroin when they were teenagers 30 and 40 years ago. Not only did the drugs they took as they were protesting made-up issues in the streets and occupying buildings in the colleges they were attending affect their minds, but also as Diana West pointed out, that affected their personalities and made them **perpetual adolescents**.

The Bible makes it clear that there is a tremendous difference between knowledge and wisdom, and many of these doctors have personalities that have not developed properly because they are still leaving God out of their lives and listening to rock.

Music and Opioids

The third thing the NIH did not recognize is that the rock 'n' roll that many of them still listen to is in itself addicting. As mentioned earlier, good music follows exact mathematical rules, which cause the mind to feel comforted, encouraged, and 'safe.' Musicians have found that when they go against these rules, the listener experiences an addicting high.

The parallels between what rock 'n' roll does to listeners and what opioids do are striking. If anyone reading this knows a teenager, or perhaps an immature adult who is rebelling against God, there is almost always something revealing about that person. He, or she, likes rock music.

As in all addictions, victims become tolerant. As noted above, opioids lead to heroin and further addiction. This is also true in music. The same music that once created a pleasant tingle of excitement no longer satisfies. The music must become more jarring, louder, and more discordant. One starts with soft rock, then rock 'n' roll, then on up to heavy metal. This has also been shown to be true of CCM. It is always just one small step behind the secular rock 'n' roll.

CCM

Not only is rock music addictive, it also does damage to one's physical, emotional and spiritual wellbeing. This was the conclusion of the American Medical Association study where they linked rock music to destructive behaviors and influences. They said in their report in 1989 and again in 2014, entitled "Adolescents and Their Music" published by the Journal of the American Medical Association: "Doctors should be alert to the listening habits of young patients as a clue to their emotional health, because fascination with rock 'n roll, especially heavy metal music, may be associated with drug use, premarital sex and satanic rites… The committee said that there is 'evidence linking involvement with rock culture with low school achievement, drugs, sexual activity and even satanic activities.' At the very least, commitment to a rock subculture is symptomatic of adolescent alienation."[1]

---

1 Brown, Elizabeth F, and William R Hendee. "Adolescents and Their Music. Insights into the Health of Adolescents." *JAMA: The Journal of the American Medical Association*, vol. 262, no. 12, 22 Sept. 1989, jamanetwork.com/journals/jama/article-abstract/378751.

Notice, please, that these quotes are not from Christians who are trying to show the problems with rock music. They are from secular audiologists and medical doctors who are trying to protect people from things that will harm them. Remember what Jesus said in Luke 16:8: "The children of this world are *in their generation* wiser than the children of light." The world says the loud rock music is harmful, but some Christians say "it is not as bad as the world says it is, so we can use that same music for the Lord." How illogical and unwise can people who call themselves Christians be?! But this is exactly what rock music has done to the thinking of *The Rock Generation* during the last six decades.

Anyone who wants to know God's mind in the area of music can readily find it by reading His Word. With at least 500 references to music in the Bible, and the availability of Bibles today, twenty-first century man cannot claim ignorance of this subject. As the Apostle Peter says "they willingly are ignorant" (II Peter 3:5), and the Apostle Paul says "they are without excuse" (Romans 1:20) concerning the things of God and His Word. **There is a "Theology of Music" in the Bible!**

HISTORY

A revealing study was reported in *The Washington Times* on October 6, 2016. In that study of forty leading universities it was discovered that over 92% of the professors over thirty-five years of age are liberal democrats. The article attributes the "race protests and the disinvitation of conservative speakers" to the universities on the overwhelming number of liberal professors influencing the policies of the present generation of students. It is also revealing that the department that has the largest percentage of liberal democrats is the **history department: over 97%.**[1]

A study of history will also reveal the battle that has existed between the world's philosophy and those who follow the teaching that the Lord has revealed through His Word. God has also revealed His will through the macrocosm of His universe and the microcosm that modern science reveals through the tools that are now available. (An excellent book titled

---

1 Richardson, Bradford. "Liberal Professors Outnumber Conservatives Nearly 12 to 1, Study Finds." *The Washington Times*, 6 Oct. 2016, www.washingtontimes.com/news/2016/oct/6/liberal-professors-outnumber-conservatives-12-1/.

More Than Meets the Eye by Richard Swenson, M.D. opens new vistas that are currently being explored.[2]) Dr. Swenson is not only a medical doctor; he is also a bio-physicist.

As far back as Pythagoras, Plato, Augustine, and Boethius, scholars and theologians recognized that patterns of music in the physical world could be traced to God through His creation. The belief in the musical harmony of the cosmic order can also be seen, and alluded to, in the works of Shakespeare, Milton, and Dryden, who included Biblical quotes in their works.

In each of these previous eras, it is not difficult to find sensual music that existed for the entertainment of guests at dinner parties and places of ill repute. Aristotle went so far as to say: "If one listens to the wrong kind of music, he will become the wrong kind of person. If he listens to the right kind of music, he will tend to become the right kind of person." This thinking was reiterated in the twentieth century by Howard Hanson, the director of the Eastman School of Music for almost 50 years. He said, "Music can be philosophical or orgiastic. It has powers for evil as well as for good." The battle that Christians are facing today is not a new one. It is as old as mankind.

---

2 Swenson, Richard A. *More than Meets the Eye: Fascinating Glimpses of God's Power and Design*. NavPress, 2000.

ALCOHOLISM

However, there are elements of the new battle that have intensified their effects. One element that proliferated in the twentieth century and is still with us in the twenty-first century is the promotion of alcoholic drinks that have accompanied worldly music wherever it appears. Fifty years ago, alcoholic use was rejected by all Christians. Today, it is accepted by many who call themselves Christians, even though the statistics should tell them how bad it is.

Many Christians do not realize that the word that is translated "sobriety" in the Bible is not talking about alcohol. The Greek word is σωφρονος (sophronos) that means "soundness of mind" or more literally "common sense." Even the world recognizes that alcohol consumption is a tremendous conundrum causing problems wherever it is consumed, even though they seem to be unwilling to do anything about it.

For instance, in the United States, according to the 2015 SAMSHA (Substance Abuse and Mental Health Services

Administration) data,[1] 15.1 million adults ages 18 and older had Alcohol Use Disorder, and an estimated 623,000 adolescents ages 12–17 had AUD; an estimated 88,000 people die from alcohol-related causes annually, making alcohol the fourth leading preventable cause of death in the United States. Globally, in 2012, over three million deaths were attributable to alcohol consumption. And in 2014, the World Health Organization reported that alcohol contributed to more than 200 diseases and injury related health conditions, liver cirrhosis, cancers, and injuries.[2]

The National Institute on Alcohol Abuse and Alcoholism states that 24.6 percent of people ages 18 and older indulge in binge drinking every month and 88,000 die from alcohol-related causes annually.[3] Teen alcohol use kills 4,700 teens each year—more than all illegal drugs combined.[4] A quick perusal of just rock group names reveals the relationship of rock and alcohol: "Creedence Clearwater Revival" ("Clearwater" is high alcohol content beer); "Everclear" was named after 190 proof grain alcohol used to make dangerous alcoholic drinks. A look at their songs will reveal their polluted mindset that has affected many teens through their songs.

1 Center for Behavioral Health Statistics and Quality. (2016), *Key Substance Use and Mental Health Indicators in the United States: Results from the 2015 National Survey on Drug Use and Health*, www.samhsa.gov/data/.

2 World Health Organization, *Global Status Report on Alcohol and Health 2014*, www.who.int/substance_abuse/publications/global_alcohol_report/.

3 "Alcohol Facts and Statistics." *National Institute on Alcohol Abuse and Alcoholism*, June 2017, www.niaaa.nih.gov/alcohol-health/ overview-alcohol-consumption/alcohol-facts-and-statistics.

4 "Fact Sheets - Underage Drinking." *Centers for Disease Control and Prevention*, 20 Oct. 2016, www.cdc.gov/ alcohol/fact-sheets/underage-drinking.htm.

DRUGS

The second element that has permeated rock music and the generation it has spawned is the acceptance of and addiction to drugs. Here are the names of just a few of the rock groups that indicate this emphasis: "Blue Cheer," a 1960's nickname for high-quality LSD; "Doobie Brothers," 1960's slang for a marijuana joint; "Motorhead," British slang for a drug user; and "Lovin' Spoonful," a drug reference to the spoon used to heat and melt heroin. A song that fooled many Christians was "Bridge Over troubled Water." The "silver girl" that is supposed to take away all your sorrow is a metaphor for the silver needle that is used to shoot heroin straight.

FREE SEX AND ABORTION

The third element that has been amplified by rock groups and has been made greater through their influence is free sex and it's attending correlation, abortion. The "groupies" that followed the Beatles, the Rolling Stones, the Who, and other similar groups all knew they could get abortions after their promiscuous escapades with their idols. It is appalling to even consider how depraved the free love songs were, and still are, with their depictions of sexuality and pornography along with profanity. However, one statistic done in 2009, and cited in 2011, should suffice: every year since 1965, ninety-two percent of all of *Billboard's Top Ten Songs* (both R&B an Pop Songs), have had "over 10 sex-related phrases per song."[1]

---

1 Hobbs, Dawn R., and Gordon G. Gallup. "Songs as a Medium for Embedded Reproductive Messages." Evolutionary Psychology, vol. 9, no. 3, 1 July 2011, doi.org/10.1177/147470491100900309.

PUNK LIFESTYLE

The fourth element that has infected the Rock Generation, and at the same time has spilled over to the CCM Generation, is drug abuse and the punk lifestyle. A perusal of the lifestyles of the rock groups for the last six decades reveals a horrific trail of drug abuse that has destroyed lives and families through rebellion, debauchery, and immorality. Even books that promote their lifestyle must admit to this with statements like: "emotional instability because of self-destructive behavior;" "live for the moment and let the rest take care of itself;" "an intoxicated sixteen-year-old;" "coffee laced with LSD-25;" "a frequent tripper" and "a turbulent, physically damaging lifestyle."[1] This lifestyle has resulted in the death by drug overdose and suicide of a large number of rock performers.

---

1 Friedlander, Paul, and Peter Miller. *Rock & Roll: a Social History*. Westview Press, 2006.

WITHOUT NATURAL AFFECTION

This has been accompanied by the proliferation of homo-sexuality that was promoted by Glam Rock and groups like "The Twisted Sister." They preferred to be called Heavy Metal but their cross-dressing and their androgyny strongly identified them and told young people they could be any sex they wanted to be. As II Timothy 3:3 says, they are "without natural affection."

The performers just mentioned go beyond boundries to include *"The Beetles" "Madonna,"* and *"Lady Gaga."* One organization that calls itself the "Acclaimed Music Forums" has over fifty pages of LGBT songs that include over three hundred perverted songs.

However, as difficult as it is to believe, even some Christian organizations have approved groups that promote homosexuality. Wheaton College gave approval to an LGBT student group on February 22, 2013,[1] and Fuller Theological Seminary followed suit on July 22, 2013.[2] The founders of both of those institutions would have been appalled at even the consideration of such an unbiblical group. The president of Fuller said the school welcomes "the opportunity to engage over vigorous issues of debate within the church and within culture." Pray tell me, *what is there to debate?!*

1 Christian Sister. "Wheaton College Provides 'Refuge' for Same-Sex Attracted Students." *ChicagoNow*, 22 Feb. 2013, www.chicagonow.com/ daily-miracle/2013/02/wheaton-college-refuge-same-sex-attracted-students/.

2 "Fuller Theological Seminary President Issues Statement about LGBT Campus Group." *Relevant Magazine*, 22 July 2013, relevantmagazine.com/slices/fuller-theological-seminary-president-issues-statement-about-lgbt-campus-group.

SUICIDE

Another incredulous subject that the songs of *The Rock Generation* have promoted through rock music is the encouragement of suicide. There are at least 150 songs that have proliferated since the year 2000 that have a distorted view of life and attempt to glorify what is a horrendous problem.[3] This has included songs of "The Grateful Dead," "Metallica," and even Bob Dylan. It is alarming to read how many superstars of rock have died from drug overdose and suicide during the last six decades.

An encouraging counter to this trend is that Christians like Oakland Raiders NFL quarterback Derek Carr, through a video on the internet that has had over four million viewers,[4] are trying to stem the tide. At a service where he spoke, Derek said God led him to ask if anyone there was contemplating suicide. He then said, "I'm here to tell you that Jesus loves

---

3 "Songs about Suicide." *Songfacts*, www.songfacts.com/category-songs_about_suicide.php. Accessed 3 March 2018.

4 "This NFL Quarterback (Derek Carr) Is Spirit-Filled!" *Holy Spirit Lifestyle*, 29 July 2017, www.facebook.com/holyspiritlifestyle/videos/1888936851375051/.

you, that I love you, and I want to pray with you and help you." Three people responded and were helped. May God give this generation more young men like Derek who are sensitive to God's leading and have the courage to speak out about it.

COMPROMISE

Churches that used to be fundamental, Bible-believing churches have abandoned hymnbooks in favor of PowerPoint presentations. Congregations no longer sing the hymns, and the people no longer have the hymnbooks with the hymns to sing in their homes. Music is one of the ways God intended as a tool for His people to meditate on His Word. When churches sing good hymns over and over, the Biblical truth they contain becomes a major part of their thinking and actions. Many good hymns have direct quotes from the Bible and become a great way to memorize Scripture, because the melody helps recall the truth of the words.

Biblical doctrine has been discarded in favor of a man-made philosophy that superimposes itself over the Bible. Any man-made system, such as hyper-Calvinism, takes people away from the truth of the Word of God and exalts man, making him arrogant. It destroys soul-winning, dries up vibrant worship, and causes churches to lose their faithful members and some churches to be closed. CCM could now be called Contemporary Calvinistic Music or Contemporary Charismatic Music.

These elements and many more continue into the twenty-first century in an accelerated fashion. Abortions are being performed at an alarming rate. Homosexuality has increased so that same-sex marriage is accepted and legalized. Colleges have become hotbeds for liberalism and rebellion, and Washington, D.C. has the highest rate of alcohol addiction of any city in the United States.[1] Not all of this can be attributed to rock music and its influence, but *The Rock Generation* has surely been a factor in promoting a philosophy through its music that is not only unbiblical but anti-biblical as well.

1 "District Columbia (DC) Alcoholism Treatment Centers." *National Alcoholism Center*, www.alcoholalcoholism.org/states/district-columbia-dc-alcoholism-treatment-centers. Accessed 22 March 2018.

MENTAL INTOXICATION

The Rock Generation has obviously contributed to the desensitization of the evil that surrounds us today. As Neil Postman made clear in *Amusing Ourselves to Death*, repeated stimulants eventually lead to tolerance, then to dissatisfaction, and finally to boredom. It takes more and more evil to relieve the boredom that accompanies overstimulation, which is exactly what rock music has done. It has over-stimulated even some Christians by its worldliness, so that what is really true, honest, just, pure, lovely, of good report, virtuous and praise worthy no longer satisfies them. They need to be amused and "intoxicated" by the things that the world can offer. CCM, by its loud volume, its emphasis on the rock beat and driving rhythm, leads to mental intoxication, and has definitely contributed to the boredom that is controlling so many minds.

The prevailing attitude and statements of the whole movement are meant to take away Biblical Truth and substitute a counterfeit religion that emphasizes the senses and the desire for excitement. Prayer and Bible study are too boring and CCM replaces true Christianity with a false sense and complete misunderstanding of who God is and what He requires of those who desire to worship Him.

GENERATION Z:
THE FRUIT OF THE ROCK GENERATION

In Matthew 12:33, the Lord Jesus Christ makes a strong statement that reinforces what He said many times. In this verse where He uses the word "fruit" three times, He summarizes with these words: "*The tree is known by its fruit.*" What follows here reveals what the fruit of *The Rock Generation* has done to the teenagers of the 21st century. The survey is titled: "Only four out of 100 teenagers have a true biblical worldview." This survey manifestly reveals the fruit of the decline that has occurred during the last six decades.

January 23, 2018— Members of Generation Z, the youngest segment of America, are at least twice as likely as American adults to identify as LGBT (lesbian, gay, bisexual, and transgender) or as atheist. While the latest Gallup Poll reported only 4.1 percent of Americans identify as LGBT, Barna found that 12 percent of Gen Z teens described their sexual orientation as something other than heterosexual, with 7 percent identifying as bisexual. Additionally, about a third of teens know someone who is transgender, and the majority (69%) say it's acceptable to be born one gender and to feel like another.[1]

January 24, 2018— A survey from the Barna Research Group found that: "Teenagers who are part of Generation Z (born from 1999 to 2015) are ***the most non-Christian generation in US history***. The survey found that more teens today identify themselves as atheist, agnostic, or not religious affiliated … Gen Z is different because they have grown up in a post-Christian, post-modern environment where many of them have not even been exposed to Christianity or to church … There are a lot of churches that are empty in this country. Gen Z is the one who is really showing the fruit of that."[2]

---

1 Shellnutt, Kate. "Get Ready, Youth Group Leaders: Teens Twice as Likely to Identify as Atheist or LGBT." *Christianity Today*, 23 Jan. 2018, www.christianitytoday.com/news/2018/january/youth-group-leaders-generation-z-atheist-lgbt-teens-barna.html.

2 Smith, Samuel. "Gen Z Is the Least Christian Generation in American History, Barna Finds." *The Christian Post*, 24 Jan. 2018, www.christianpost.com/news/gen-z-is-the-least-christian-generation-in-american-history-barna-finds-214856/.

"SOCIAL PROMOTION"

What follows is an idea that was promoted in public schools many years ago (mainly the 1930's), and it is one of the primary problems with public schools today. Social promotion is the practice of promoting a child to the next grade level regardless of skill mastery in the belief that it will promote self-esteem. It moves a student to the next grade after the current school year, regardless of when or whether they didn't learn the necessary materials or they are often absent, in order to keep them with their peers.

In the past, this was only done with individual students. In Washington D.C., however, as with almost everything else there, the mental intoxication of the Rock Generation carries a bad idea to the extreme. A current example demonstrates how far off the tree the fruit of *The Rock Generation* has fallen. This news organization reports on an alarming trend in Washington, D.C., our nation's illustrious capital, where the federal government and the national media display their inefficiency and inability to think logically when they leave God out of the equation.

January 17, 2018— OneNewsNow: Every single student—including students who do not show up for class for months and cannot read or write—received their diplomas at Ballou High School in Washington, D.C. This liberal graduation trend is by no means a rare occurrence on high school campuses in the nation's capital.[1]

Students across the city graduated despite having missed more than 30 days of school in a single course, findings from the D.C. Office of the State Superintendent investigation found. All 164 seniors at Ballou received diplomas—with dozens of them issued to students with excessively high rates of unexcused absences—and to top that off, every single graduate of the school applied to college and was accepted. This marvel—in an area of the nation that was amongst the lowest in high school graduation rates for years—was celebrated and covered by national media across the nation.

The vacuum that the "Christian" segment of The Rock Generation has created is being filled by the rise of Islam in many countries including the United States of America. Dr. Gene Gurganus has written a very enlightening book titled *Islam, Past, Present, Future: What Every American Needs to Know.*[2] This book sheds light on an impending calamity that is coming to America where some estimates say that many Americans convert to Islam every year. Listen to what

---

1 Haverluck, Michael F. "Illiterates, No-Shows, All Seniors Graduate at DC High." *OneNewsNow*, 17 Jan. 2018, www.onenewsnow.com/education/2018/01/17/illiterates-no-shows-all-seniors-graduate-at-dc-high.

2 Gurganus, Gene. *Islam Past, Present, Future: What Every Loyal American Needs to Know.* Truth Publishers, 2011.

this missionary to Muslims for many years says on page 22 in a section called "America Is in Trouble."

> *Think with me of the breakdown of the family: alcoholism, drug addiction, sexual abuse, violence and a media, both TV and the internet, oozing with unbridled sexual content. Not only is that true, but the church in America is in trouble. The church of Jesus Christ is not healthy … Neo-evangelicalism is no longer evangelical. Christian fundamentalists view each other with suspicion. The super churches are no longer soul-winning churches with bus routes. Seeker friendly churches giving people what they want instead of what they need are biggies today. Instead of the church going into the world with the Gospel, the world is coming into the church with entertainment.*

CHRIST IS THE ANSWER

Those who know the Lord realize that He is the only One who can solve the problems that have been brought on so intensively by The Rock Generation. We also know that He will solve them someday when He comes to rule and reign in the millennium that has been prophesied in the Bible (Revelation 20:3-6). Meanwhile, we should do everything we can by being faithful in witnessing, praying, and holding back the evil that those who don't know our Savior are promoting so vigorously. The gospel of Jesus Christ is the message that has made western civilization different from the rest of the world, and the proclamation and acceptance of its message is the only thing that will keep our country from becoming like the rest of the world.

Nominal and notional Christians think they have found the truth while they have adopted a perversion of the truth that the Bible condemns. For instance, Galatians 1:6-7 warns us that there are false teachers who "change the gospel of Christ into another gospel" because they "pervert the gospel of Christ." Also, Second Corinthians 11:3-4 warns that there are some who "preach another Jesus." Each Christian must be certain to have a close, personal relationship with the Lord Himself that manifests itself in all that we say and do. ***Faith is only as valid as the object of that faith.***

GOOD EXAMPLES FROM THE BIBLE

This little book would not be complete without some encouragement from the Word of God. The best way to do this is to use illustrations from Bible characters who have impacted their generations by being faithful to Him in the wicked society where God called them.

JOSEPH

The first illustration that comes to mind is **Joseph**. God called him to Egypt where Joseph said, "God hath caused me to be fruitful in the **land of my affliction**." The thing that made Joseph fruitful in that ungodly place was that he brought GOD into every situation where he found himself: With Potiphar's wife, with the butler and baker in Prison, with Pharaoh (he mentioned God four times), with his brothers the first time they came before him to buy grain, with his steward (who mentions God twice to the brothers), with his brothers again (Joseph mentions God four times when he reveals himself to them), and then to his brothers four more times when he says "God meant it for good," and "God will visit you." Israel was safe in Egypt for the next two hundred years because of Joseph's faithfulness.

RAHAB AND RUTH

The second illustration that comes to mind is about two women, **Rahab** and **Ruth**. Both of these women are remarkable examples of following whatever light they had, which must have been small, and letting God use them to accomplish His will. Most people do not realize the relationship between these two women who followed God in spite of the immoral circumstances in which they were brought up. In the Bible Rahab is called "Rahab the Harlot" four times, including Hebrews 11:31 where she is an example of faith. The reason she is called that was that she was more than likely a temple prostitute for the wicked Canaanite priests in Jericho. However, that did not keep her from helping the spies and eventually becoming the grandmother of Obed and the great-great grandmother of King David.

Ruth was a Moabite. Where did the Moabites come from? It was from a horrible, illicit relationship between Lot's firstborn daughter and himself. To put it mildly, Ruth had a terrible background. The Moabites worshipped Astoreth, the goddess of the Zidonians and Chemosh who was their god. The young women of Moab were taught that if they could have a child by one of their wicked priests, they could offer that child as a sacrifice to their god. (Abortion is nothing new.)

But Ruth, unlike her sister-in-law Orpah, turned from Moabite idols to the Living God. Her dedication recorded in the book with her name (Ruth 1:16-17) is almost unbelievable for a girl with her background, including "thy people shall be my people, and thy God my God." As a result she became the wife of Boaz (Rahab's and Salmon's son), the mother of Obed, the great-grandmother of King David, and along with Rahab, is mentioned by Matthew in the line of Christ (Matthew 1:5-6 where both women are named, and Luke 3:31-32, where only men are named).

ESTHER

The third illustration is also about a woman, **Esther**. She was brought to the "house of the women" according to the law of the iniquitous Medes and Persians as a possible candidate to be the wife of Ahasuerus the king. Her uncle, Mordecai, who had brought her up as his own child, told her not to let people know she was a Jew. She was actually to be just one of the king's concubines, but in God's providence Ahasuerus loved her and made her the queen.

When wicked Haman, the Agagite, saw that Mordecai would not "reverence" him, he sought to have Mordecai and all the Jews killed. When word of this was brought to Esther, she was caught in a quandary because she knew she could not come before the king without his special permission. Then emanates the special admonition of Mordecai to his niece: "Who knoweth whether thou art come to the kingdom for such a time as this?" Esther's marvelous reply is, "I will go in unto the king, which is not according to the law; and **if I perish, I perish**." The rest of the story tells how God worked out everything because of Esther's faithfulness in obeying and serving Him.

DANIEL

The fourth illustration is **Daniel**. The Bible does not reveal what tribe of Israel he came from. He was not a priest but the son of royalty and he was made a eunuch by the Chaldeans when he was taken to Babylon. In spite of that humiliating circumstance, "he purposed in his heart not to defile himself" by the customs of the wicked society in which he found himself. This gave him opportunities, but with the opportunities came problems.

Many Christians want the victories without the trials. That was not Daniel's life or experience. His three companions had to go into the fiery furnace before they could be delivered out. Daniel had to go into the lion's den before God could save his life by closing the lions' mouths. He had to put his life in the hand of the wicked king before he could deliver the message God gave him. However, he never flinched nor compromised his testimony in any circumstance.

Chapter six of the book of Daniel says that "when the writing was signed" that meant certain death, Daniel "went into his house; and his windows being open in his chamber toward Jerusalem, he kneeled upon his knees three times a day, and prayed, and gave thanks before his God, as he did aforetime." God used Daniel to not only affect his generation in a positive way, but He allowed Daniel to prophecy things that are being fulfilled now and things that are yet to come.

THE APOSTLE PAUL

The fifth and last illustration is from the New Testament, the **Apostle Paul**. He was a Pharisee of the Pharisees who tried to extinguish Christianity, even witnessing the martyrdom of Stephen. However, "breathing out threatenings and slaughter against the disciples of the Lord," he met the Savior on the Road to Damascus and was completely changed. As an ambassador for Christ, he was opposed every step of the way. But he remained faithful through every trial he faced: opposition, prison, persecution, stripes, stoning, beatings with rods, and many other "perils."

Paul said in Romans 8:28, "And we know that all things work together for good to them that love God, to them who are the called according to His purpose." Of all the things he faced, there is one that stands as one that can be applied to everything else that has been noted in this book. When Paul was standing before King Agrippa and Festus, they said he could have been freed if he had not appealed to Caesar. This meant he had to go to Rome.

CHAINED TO PAUL

The book of Acts mentions several times that there was a "soldier," a guard "that kept him" as a prisoner all the way. In other words, Paul was constantly (except for a few moments as when there was a shipwreck at Melita), chained to a special soldier who was part of Caesar's most-trusted Legion called the Praetorian Guard. These elite soldiers all seemed to have the rank of Centurion, but they were Paul's "captive audience" because Paul was not only chained to them, **they were chained to Paul**.

If you have studied and know the apostle Paul, you know that he must have witnessed to each of those men and won many of them to the Lord. At least, each soldier must have heard this Roman citizen witness to others, or pray and sing praises to God. The book of Philippians reveals two places where Paul mentions these men. In Philippians 1:13 Paul says: "My bonds in Christ are manifest in all the palace" (Caesar's Court). Verse 14 seems to imply that many of these men ("the brethren in the Lord") became confident and bold "to speak the word without fear."

Then in Philippians 4:22, Paul says: "All the saints salute you, chiefly they that are of Caesar's household" (his Imperial Civil Service). This elite group had members all over the world at that time. They were palace officials, secretaries, and others who conducted the affairs of the Roman Empire, and the Apostle Paul called them saints. It is not exaggerating to say that many of these men must have been led to Christ for Paul to call them saints!

THE WHITE HOUSE

Apply this to NOW! The news has reported that in August of 2017 a weekly Bible study is being held in the White House for the first time in at least 100 years. About a dozen members of the Trump Cabinet attend, including President Donald Trump and Vice President Mike Pence.

Ralph Drollinger, the organizer, is a former National Basketball Association player who has formed Capitol Ministries that holds Bible studies in 40 state capitols and a number of foreign capitols. Drollinger's comment about the White House Bible study fits right in with what happened to the Praetorian Guard: "I don't think Donald Trump has figured out that he chained himself to [an] **Apostle Paul**."[1] It appears that Mike Pence might be discipling Donald Trump.

It is also encouraging to discover that as of March 10, 2018, Ralph Reed, the chairman of the "Faith and Freedom

---

1 Wishon, Jennifer. "Bible Studies at the White House: Who's Inside This Spiritual Awakening?" *The Christian Broadcasting Network*, 31 July 2017, www1.cbn.com/cbnnews/politics/2017/july/bible-studies-at-the-white-house-whos-at-the-heart-of-this-spiritual-awakening.

Coalition" has established the "Trump Prayer Team." He is seeking to build a 10-million prayer team to pray daily that "President Trump will be granted wisdom, knowledge, and understanding, that he will be given godly counsel and God-fearing advisors, and that he will work to reverse the trends of Godless secular humanism."

All American Christians are obligated to pray for their government, but as we rejoice in what is happening in the White House, we should be certain that every one of us is fulfilling God's calling and will for each of us. If Joseph, Rahab, Ruth, Esther, Daniel, and Paul did it in their Generation, we can do it as we live in *The Rock Generation*.

Can Rock Music Be Sacred?

The booklet *Can Rock Music Be Sacred?* was written and published in 1974. It is a succinct, straight-forward, hard-hitting, biblically-based book that appears to be prophetic in describing not only what was transpiring the second decade of the Rock Generation, but what is still coming to pass in the sixth decade, 2010-2020. *Can Rock Music be Sacred?* is essential reading for anyone who wants to recognize the decline that began in the 1960's and that has intensified over the last forty-three years.

At the time this book is being published, *Can Rock Music be Sacred?* is being revised and updated for republication. It is scheduled to be published in 2018 by Sierra Creation in print and ebook format.

"No New Thing Under the Sun"

In the book of Ecclesiastes "The Preacher" says, "There is no new thing under the sun. Is there anything whereof it may be said, See, this is new? It hath been already of old time, which was before us" (Ecclesiastes 1:9-10). The following are two illustrations that will demonstrate how what has been written in this book describing *The Rock Generation* is not new. The first illustration is from two hundred twenty years ago, and the second one is from one hundred thirty years ago. The first illustration involves three men of the 18th century.

The first of the three is William Wilberforce (1759-1833), who wrote a 399-page treatise in 1797 that has the title: *A Practical View of the Prevailing Religious System of Professed Christians in the Higher and Middle Class in this Country, Contrasted with REAL CHRISTIANITY.* (Book titles in those days were long!) This politician, who was instrumental in eradicating slavery from England, was also a devout Bible-believing Christian who opposed the compromise of the "rock generation" of the eighteenth century. Abraham Lincoln said that "everyone should know about Wilberforce."

The second is John Newton (1725-1807), a former salve trader who became a Christian and wrote the song that is still the most popular hymn of all time; "Amazing Grace." That song is still sung more than any other hymn. Newton developed a special relationship with Wilberforce, and through letters and contact encouraged him to oppose the slave trade that was ingrained into society at that time. Having experienced "Real Christianity," the two men produced a hymnbook and called it *Olney Hymns* after the place where they lived and worked. Bible-believing churches still sing many of the songs in *Olney Hymns*.[1]

The third is William Cowper, pronounced "Cooper" (1731-1800). Cowper was one of England's greatest poets and wrote many hymns as well, including: "God Moves in a Mysterious Way" and "There Is a Fountain Filled with Blood." Sixty-six of Cowper's hymns were in *Olney Hymns*, and they were used by God to promote the truth of the Bible through music and poetry. This coincided with Wilberforce's desire to proclaim the tenants of "Real Christianity" that all three 18th century men of different backgrounds believed and practiced.

The second illustration is about the 19th century "Prince of Preachers," Charles Haddon Spurgeon. He was strong in defending the Bible in agreement with the *1689 London Baptist Confession of Faith*. He was opposed to the compromise of the Baptist Union in the 19th century, and he liked to think of himself as a "mere Christian." He said, "I do not hesitate to take the name of Baptist, but if I am asked what is my creed, I

---

1 Newton, John, and William Cowper. *Olney Hymns*. W. Oliver, 1779.

reply, 'It is Jesus Christ.'" Like all great men of God, he made his faith in the Living Savior the center of his teaching and preaching, not any man-made system.

In what was called "The Downgrade Controversy," Spurgeon was outspoken in saying, "we are going downhill at breakneck speed." He noted that every revival of true evangelical faith had been followed within a generation or two by a drift away from sound doctrine, ultimately leading to wholesale apostasy. He was alarmed that former "fundamental" Baptist churches in England drifted from orthodoxy toward an ancient form of theological liberalism called Socinianism, or toward Arianism (which denies the full deity of Christ). Still others simply became enamored with scholarship and worldly wisdom; consequently they lost their zeal for truth.

Here is a part of what Spurgeon wrote in 1888: "Certain ministers are treacherously betraying our holy religion under pretense of adapting it to this present age. This, then, is the proposal. By semi-dramatic performances they make houses of prayer to approximate to the theatre; they turn their services into musical displays. In order to win the world, the Lord Jesus must conform himself, his people, and His Word to the world. I will not dwell on so loathsome a proposal."[2]

---

2 Spurgeon, Charles H. "No Compromise." The
   Metropolitan Tabernacle. 7 Oct. 1888.

IMITATE FANNY CROSBY

As you have read this, you are probably thinking: "What Can I do?" As a musician and a hymn-writer, I love to study those who have influenced my life and writing. One of those people was Frances Jane Crosby, better known as Fanny Crosby, who lived from 1820 to 1915.

Although Fanny was blind, she did not consider herself handicapped. She did many of the things other children did, and accepted her blindness with a positive attitude that was evident in the short poem she wrote when she was just eight years old:

Oh, what a happy soul I am,
Although I cannot see!
I am resolved that in this world
Contented I will be.
How many blessings I enjoy
That other people don't,
To weep and sigh because I'm blind
I cannot, and I won't!

This poet who was blind since she was six weeks old wrote somewhere between 8,000 and 9,000 hymns. The best-known one is probably "Blessed Assurance, Jesus Is Mine." However, the thing I want to mention here is what Fanny had put on her tombstone in Bridgeport, Connecticut:

"SHE HATH DONE WHAT SHE COULD"

Let's all do the same!!

Selected Bibliography

Begbie, Jeremy S. *Resounding Truth: Christian Wisdom in the World of Music*. Baker Academic, 2007.

Blanchard, John, and Dan Lucarini. *Can We Rock the Gospel?: Rock Music's Impact on Worship and Evangelism*. Evangelical Press, 2006.

Blesser, Barry. *The Seductive (Yet Destructive) Appeal of Loud Music*. 2007, www.blesser.net/downloads/ eContact%20Loud%20Music.pdf.

Bloom, Allan. *The Closing of the American Mind*. Simon and Schuster, 1987.

Boice, James Montgomery. *Sure I Believe - so What!* Christian Focus, 2003.

Brokaw, Tom. *The Greatest Generation Speaks: Letters and Reflections*. Random House Trade Paperbacks, 2001.

Cooke, Deryck. *Language of Music*. Oxford University Press, 1959.

Everson, Dana. *Sound Roots: Steps to Building a Biblical Philosophy of Music*. Bible Revival Ministries, 2008.

Garlock, Frank, and Kurt Woetzel. *Music in the Balance*. Majesty Music, 1992.

Garlock, Frank. *Can Rock Music Be Sacred?* Majesty Music, 2018.

Gurganus, Gene, *Islam, Past, Present, Future: What Every American Needs to Know.* Truth Publishers, 2011.

Hamilton, Shelly. *Why I Don't Listen to Contemporary Christian Music.* Majesty Music, 2013.

Hines, Jerome. *This Is My Story, This Is My Song.* Fleming H. Revell, 1963.

Howard, Pierce J. *The Owner's Manual for the Brain: Everyday Applications from Mind-Brain Research.* Bard Press, 2006.

Hughes, R. Kent. *Set Apart: Calling a Worldly Church to a Godly Life.* Crossway Books, 2003.

Hunt, Arthur W. *Vanishing Word: the Veneration of Visual Imagery in the Postmodern World.* Wipf & Stock Publishers, 2013.

Johnson, Julian. *Who Needs Classical Music?: Cultural Choice and Musical Value.* Oxford University Press, 2011.

Jones, Paul S. *Singing and Making Music: Issues in Church Music Today.* P&R Publishing, 2006.

Jourdain, Robert. *Music, the Brain, and Ecstasy: How Music Captures Our Imagination.* William Morrow Paperbacks, 1997.

Key, Wilson Bryan. *Subliminal Seduction.* Berkley, 1974.

Lucarini, Dan. *It's Not About the Music.* EP Books, 2010.

McLuhan, Marshall, and Quentin Fiore. *The Medium Is the Massage: an Inventory of Effects.* Penguin Books, 1967.

Miell, Dorothy, et al. *Musical Communication.* Oxford University Press, 2005.

Pattison, Robert. *The Triumph of Vulgarity: Rock Music in the Mirror of Romanticism.* Oxford University Press, 1987.

Plantinga, Cornelius. *Not the Way It's Supposed to Be: a Breviary of Sin.* Eerdmans, 1996.

Postman, Neil. *Amusing Ourselves to Death: Public Discourse in the Age of Showbusiness.* Penguin Books, 2005.

Reich, Charles A. *The Greening of America.* Crown Trade Paperbacks, 1995.

Smith, Kimberly. *Music and Morals: Dispelling the Myth That Music Is Amoral.* Capella Books, 2006.

Swenson, Richard A. *More than Meets the Eye: Fascinating Glimpses of God's Power and Design.* NavPress, 2000.

Tame, David. *The Secret Power of Music.* Destiny Books, 1984.

West, Diana. *The Death of the Grown-up: How America's Arrested Development Is Bringing down Western Civilization.* St. Martin's Griffin, 2008.

Wiersbe, Warren W. *William Culbertson: a Man of God.* Moody Press, 1974.

Wolf, Garen L. *Church Music Matters: a Music Philosophy in Christian Perspective*. Schmul Publishing, 2005.

Wolf, Garen L. *Music of the Bible in Christian Perspective: a Biblically Historic Study of Music from Antiquity, with Philosophical Application to Twenty-First Century Church Music*. Schmul Publishing, 1996.

53300806R00057

Made in the USA
Columbia, SC
15 March 2019